This book belongs to

_____

Barbie™
in
Princess Golden-Hood

Illustrations by
Lawrence Mann

EGMONT

EGMONT

We bring stories to life

First published in Great Britain 2008
by Egmont UK Limited
239 Kensington High Street, London W8 6SA

ISBN 978 1 4052 3848 9

1 3 5 7 9 10 8 6 4 2

Printed in Germany

Hello, I'm Amelia, Princess of Arcadia.

This is a story about what happened when I met Mr Wolf on my way to Granny's cottage. The poor wolf had to learn a lesson about greediness . . .

On Princess Amelia's birthday, her beloved grandmother gave her a wonderful golden cape lined with silk and satin.

The cape had a hood to keep off the sun and rain, and it suited the princess down to the ground.

Amelia loved her cape so much that she wore it wherever she went. Soon everyone nicknamed her Princess Golden-Hood.

A few days after Amelia's birthday, Granny invited her to tea. Amelia was very excited. She loved to spend time with her grandmother.

Amelia and her mother, the Queen, filled a basket with jellies, cupcakes and sweets, and the Queen sent Princess Golden-Hood happily on her way, but with a warning.

"Stay on the path, my child, for the wood contains dangers untold," the Queen said in a hushed voice.

As Amelia skipped along the path with her pet dog, Truffle, her golden cape sparkled and shone in the bright sunlight.

The princess looked as pretty as a picture as she picked the flowers that grew in the long grass. Truffle scampered this way and that, chasing butterflies that fluttered around the tip of his nose.

Suddenly, Amelia realised that Truffle had strayed from the path!

"Truffle! Truffle! Come back here!" Amelia called, running after the little dog, who disappeared through the trees until he was out of sight.

By the time Amelia caught up with him, they'd wandered so far from the path they were quite lost.

"Now look at what you've done, Truffle! We've left the path and we'll be late for tea with Granny," Amelia told the little dog, all the time cuddling him to let him know she wasn't angry.

Princess Golden-Hood had not noticed the wolf watching her from behind a tree.

Mr Wolf had been taking a leisurely stroll when Amelia's golden cape caught his eye and the smell of delicious treats reached his greedy snout.

"What is Princess Golden-Hood doing here in the woods?" Mr Wolf wondered. "And what does she have in her basket?"

As Amelia came closer, Mr Wolf stepped out in front of her and tipped his cap politely. "Good afternoon, fair princess," he said, surprising Amelia.

"Where are you going, Princess Golden-Hood?" asked the friendly wolf.

"I am taking jellies and cupcakes to my grandmother," replied Amelia sweetly. "Perhaps you would like to try one?"

Mr Wolf peered into the basket, and, with a charming smile, took one of the biggest cupcakes and gobbled it whole. "Why, thank you, princess! Where does your granny live?"

"On the other side of the woods in Castlewood Cottage, by Water-Lily Pond," said Amelia. "We are very late for our tea!"

"Please don't worry, Princess Golden-Hood," said Mr Wolf, patting her hand with his paw. "I shall run and tell your grandmother you will be late."

Mr Wolf sped to Castlewood Cottage. That cupcake had made him hungry for more!

Through the window he could see the parlour. A fire had been lit and a table had been laid with a mountain of cucumber sandwiches, slices of delicious fruit and sweet raspberry meringues.

He knocked on the door.

"I am a kindly w . . . woodcutter," he growled, "a friend of Amelia. I have a message from her!"

Hearing Amelia's name, Granny lifted the latch, and opened the cottage door.

In a flash of fur, the wolf sped across the parlour and gobbled up every last morsel of the feast!

"Oh, you greedy creature! That was our tea!" Granny gasped. "Whatever will Amelia and I eat now?"

Amelia was skipping out of the woods with Truffle scampering beside her when she heard her grandmother's shouts coming all the way from Castlewood Cottage.

"Poor Granny! She must be in danger! Whatever has that wolf done?" she cried, fleeing to the cottage, with Truffle at her heels.

Through the window, Mr Wolf caught sight of Amelia's golden cape as she approached, and he sped from the cottage, straight for Water-Lily Pond.

But the wolf was so full up with food that he lost his balance and SPLASH fell into the water!

Amelia ran to Water-Lily Pond and saw a sorry-looking wolf shivering in the shallow water, too tired and full to climb out again. She held out her hand and helped him out of the pond.

Amelia wrapped her golden cape around the wolf. The cape kept him warm as Amelia led him back to Castlewood Cottage and sat him before the roaring fire.

Granny was not pleased to see Mr Wolf again. "He gobbled up our tea!" said Granny to Amelia.

But Amelia felt pity for the poor wolf and brought him cups of hot cocoa to warm him up.

"I'm so terribly sorry for eating all your food," said Mr Wolf, feeling ashamed. "I have certainly learned my lesson, not to be so greedy!"

"We forgive you, Mr Wolf," said the princess. "Besides, I still have plenty of cupcakes, jellies and sweets in my basket!"

At long last, Amelia, Granny and Truffle could enjoy their delicious tea.

As Princess Amelia skipped home that night, Mr Wolf walked beside her. In return for Amelia's kindness, Mr Wolf promised always to look out for Princess Golden-Hood and make sure she came to no harm.

Princess Amelia and Mr Wolf became great friends and Amelia invited the wolf to each and every royal banquet held at her palace, as her guest of honour.

But Mr Wolf only ate polite portions and never devoured a whole feast ever again!